SCHOOL

Homeless PUPPY
Found Home and Stopped Bullies

by
Daniel Kotey Addison

AuthorHouse™ UK
1663 Liberty Drive
Bloomington, IN 47403 USA
www.authorhouse.co.uk
UK TFN: 0800 0148641 (Toll Free inside the UK)
UK Local: 02036 956322 (+44 20 3695 6322 from outside the UK)

Because of the dynamic nature of the Internet, any web addresses or links contained in this book may have changed
since publication and may no longer be valid. The views expressed in this work are solely those of the author and do not
necessarily reflect the views of the publisher, and the publisher hereby disclaims any responsibility for them.

Any people depicted in stock imagery provided by Getty Images are models,
and such images are being used for illustrative purposes only.
Certain stock imagery © Getty Images.

This book is printed on acid-free paper.

ISBN: 979-8-8230-8242-6 (sc)
ISBN: 979-8-8230-8241-9 (e)

Print information available on the last page.

Published by AuthorHouse 04/21/2023

authorHOUSE®

Once upon a time there was a puppy that lost her parents during a heavy rainstorm and a gusting wind.

The puppy was washed away from her parents and ended up at a nearby farmhouse, wandering about with no shelter, or food to eat.

There was a little girl called Araba, who lived in a little farmhouse with her parents Mr Ahobrase and Mrs Ahobrase, and a younger brother called Kofi. Araba always wanted a puppy but her parents always denied her to have one.

Araba's parents are from different races, Araba's dad is African descendant and her mum is an European descendant, and because both parents are from different descendance, this makes Araba and Kofi mix race children.

One"stormy" night, while Araba and her family were having dinner, they heard a sound "bang" at the door. They wondered what that "sound" could be.

Araba immediately ran to the door and found a soaking wet shivering puppy hiding at the corner of the doorway.

Araba screamed in dismay and called her younger brother, Kofi!"Kofi", come! " said Araba.

Araba's parents wondered what it was and both parents asked,

Is everything alright?

Araba then responded, "Yes, everything is fine."

Kofi rushed to the doorway and said to Araba. "What is wrong with you Araba?

Araba pointed to the corner "puppy", "Look! Can we keep it? I don't know," Kofi replied,

Then Kofi said "Ask mummy and daddy".

The puppy was soaking and wet in the rain and, Araba, was very sad to see the puppy soaked and shivering.,

Araba quickly ran to her daddy thinking she could convince her daddy to keep the puppy in the house.

Some of the African parents are not fond of pets, they think it is more responsibility and time consuming to have a pet besides your children.

Daddy" Araba called out, do you know what that noise was? No! Her daddy replied. What was that Araba, her daddy asked?.

That noise was a little wet puppy!

The puppy might be lost and I think the puppy needs a place to stay, Araba claimed.

You don't know for sure, Said her daddy!

Araba looked at her younger brother Kofi, who was waiting calmly with the puppy at the doorway.

Araba then asked her "daddy "Can I bring the puppy inside so the puppy can get some warmth.

"Ooooh Araba", her dad exaggerates and says, "I don't know.", "why don't you see what your mum thinks? "

"But daddy," Araba, added, "you know how much I've always wanted a puppy, and you always said we can't afford one."

"No no no! That's not what I meant Araba, " her dad replied.

"What did you mean daddy? Araba asked. "What I meant was that it is not easy to look after a puppy, a puppy needs special care," her daddy advised.

"How is it daddy? Araba asked reluctantly. Please daddy I love this puppy, she added. Araba had trouble convincing her parents to allow her to keep the puppy inside the house.

Araba was a very brilliant child, she always paid attention to and listened to her parents and elders in the community, she always did everything right, but yet she wasn't allowed to keep the puppy.

Araba, never argued or disobeyed anyone. Araba was very sad and disappointed because she thought a puppy would make things better and get some comfort from the puppy and forget about her peers at school who always bullied her and her younger brother.

Araba's peers often picked on her and her younger brother Kofi, when they were on their way from school or from the town, her peers often took things Araba and her younger brother Kofi carried and threw them away just to make them afraid.

Araba's (peers) even made fun of both her and her younger brother Kofi, sometimes the bullies took their book bags and tossed them across the floor in the school when there were no adults present.

The bullying was very difficult for Araba and her younger brother Kofi to deal with, they had no means to stop their peers from the horrific ordeal, and both were not ready to report it to their parents, or any adult.

Araba always wished she could have someone to stand up to her (peers) and tell them to stop bothering her and her younger brother.

Araba and her younger brother Kofi, never picked on anyone, nor they offended their peers or defended themselves as they had always been bullied by bullies.

[Meanwhile], Kofi was still watching over the puppy at the door and Araba's mum was busy washing the dishes in the kitchen.

Kofi then runs off to the bathroom and fetches a towel and a small basket from the garage. Kofi dried the puppy, placed the puppy in the basket and created a shelter with branches in the bush and hid the puppy in the bushes close to the house.

Araba was unable to convince her parents, Araba shed a few tears but she never gave up hope of taking care of the homeless shivering puppy. Araba, kind of this time she has to do any means necessary and keep the puppy safe.

Araba approached Kofi to discuss what they could do next to help the puppy survive. Fortunately, by that time, Kofi had already taken care of the problem.

Araba was excited and proud to see her younger brother taking responsibility, they stayed up with the puppy for a while to ensure the puppy was safe and warm.

"Well, Kofi is getting late, " said Araba! Let's get inside before mummy and daddy get angry, both were very sad to leave the puppy alone in the bushes near the house.

Kofi had dried up the puppy and placed the puppy in the basket, but the two siblings did not feel comfortable leaving the puppy alone in the bushes.

Araba and her younger brother, being wonderful and respectful children, felt obliged to keep the puppy safe without her parents being aware. Kofi retired to bed and slept,

but, Araba couldn't sleep that night. Araba tossed and turned in bed and peered through her window every minute to see if the puppy was okay. Araba got tired and falled asleep

The puppy! Suddenly. Araba sighed in her sleep, whilst lying in bed at night. Araba couldn't get enough sleep due to the plight of the puppy, not because the puppy was disturbing her sleep, but she felt sorry and obliged for the lonely puppy left alone in the bushes.

The next day was a Saturday and Araba woke up restless. Araba's eyes were red, puffy, a little moody and unfriendly because of her sleepless night due to the condition of the puppy.

It was a weekend so Araba and her younger brother Kofi didn't have to go to school. Araba was usually moody on school days because she had to see her disturbing peers those days.

Daddy was wondering why Araba's eyes were puffy and moody. Her daddy asked, "Are you alright Araba?

"Yes daddy" Araba responded with a lower tone of voice.

I thought you would be happy today because you didn't have to go to school. Her daddy jokes. Honestly, Araba's daddy had no idea what was going on.

Araba looked at her daddy with funny eyes and giggling and then turned towards her younger brother Kofi and signaled to him. Her daddy looked at both and smiled without knowing what the siblings had planned.

That morning, Araba and Kofi ate most of their breakfast and yet saved some for the puppy in a small plastic container and hid it.

Araba didn't want her parents to find out what she was doing with the plastic container and the food inside, Araba knows she might get into trouble with her parents if they find out she disobeyed them.

After the breakfast Araba and her younger brother Kofi popped out to the bushes where the puppy was kept whilst her daddy was getting ready to go to the farm yard and work on the field.

Araba and her younger brother Kofi, took the breakfast they had saved for the puppy and went into the bushes to feed the puppy.

The puppy was hungry and lonely the night before, the puppy tossed over and over on her bed just like Araba, but finally the puppy had some decent sleep in the basket due to the towel Kofi placed on her to give her warmth.

Though Araba's peers in school were picking on them, she never ever mentioned it to her parents, and also warned her younger brother Kofi, not to say a word to their parents, or any adults".

Both siblings somehow always get scared to step out from the house and go to the town and get groceries from the shops.

They wanted to let things out and be free from the bullying, but they were threatened by their 'peers' if they dared tell on them.

Araba thought her parents might be worried, and her peers at school would also be furious if they told their parents, or any adults about the bullies, things might get worse.

Araba and her younger brother Kofi, being wonderful kids, yet" their peers picked on them, and did all the horrible and despicable things to them.

As the days went by the puppy settled and grew, Araba and her younger brother Kofi took very good care of the puppy without their parents' knowledge, but later their parents became fond of the grown big dog when they found out the siblings had kept the puppy.

The grown dog watched over the farmyard, preventing the bush animals from destroying the crops. The dog loved to snoop around in the bushes during the day and night when no one was around.

The dog became like a wild forest animal, sometimes hunting to feed herself in the bushes, let alone keeping the bush animals away from the crops in the farm.

Araba's daddy was working on the farm one sunny after-noon when he heard a sound from the bushes. Araba's daddy thought it was the farm animals that often destroyed his crops.

Araba's daddy became alert waiting to trap the farm animals. The sound began to escalate, the bushes were heavily shaken to the length that he became a bit frightened.

Araba's daddy did not know that Araba and her younger brother Kofi had kept the puppy all this time, and was now a full grown dog. Araba's daddy stood there on the farm in a clear view ready to get hold of the farm animals.

The bushes shook extensively off the farm across and this began worrying Araba's daddy because this never happened before on the farm.

Although the bush animals were tearing down his crops, not in a slight the bushes were extensively shaked across the field consistently.

During the week, Araba and her younger brother Kofi go to school and their parents stay behind and work on the farm. That sunny after-noon Araba's mummy was inside the house doing some chores.

Araba's daddy became frightened and quickly went to the house to get a huge stick, Araba's mum seeing Araba's daddy rush into the house, Araba's mummy asked

"Are you alright my dear?"

"No!" he replied.

"What's going on darling? Araba's mummy asked.

"I don't know,"Araba's daddy responded.

There's something unusual in the bushes. I don't know what that is, Araba's daddy added.

Araba's daddy, grabbed the stick, a very large stick, and headed back to the farm, and waited in a clear area off from the bushes, where he could clearly see when the animals appeared.

As Araba's daddy was waiting, he noticed a bush animal rush out chased by a dog. Araba's daddy was very surprised to see a dog on the farm, and he also noticed his crops had been growing well for some time now.

Araba's daddy stood there with a cheerful face and smiled, and shook his head and said to himself, "Oh Araba." Araba's daddy now understood why the bushes were shaking so extensively. It was the puppy he forbade Araba from keeping and now it had grown into a big dog.

Araba's daddy called the dog but initially, the dog was a bit scared of him. Araba's daddy was friendly and gentle, eventually the dog shook her tail, and began to move little by little close to Araba's dad and the dog and Araba's dad became acquaintance.

Araba and her younger brother Kofi arrived at the farmhouse from school that very day, the dog and her daddy became acquaintances. The siblings got picked on as usual in the school. Araba and her younger brother Kofi, still kept quiet over the bullying from their parents.

When both arrived, Araba's mum had already prepared dinner for the family to sit together and eat as always. During dinner Araba's mum asked her dad about the sound he heard in the farmyard.

Araba's dad started laughing and giggling uncontrollably. "What's funny dear? hmmm," Araba's mummy asked.

Araba's dad giggled again and said, "I think I know why the crops are growing well these days in the farm."

Araba and her younger brother Kofi looked at each other and smiled. Araba then asked her daddy, "how did that happen?

"Oh" you know, Araba's daddy scratched his nose with his fingernails and said, that's our little secret, " her dad replied. "I wonder how a dog got to the farm yard" her daddy added.

"A dog on the farm yard" Araba's mum exclaimed. "How did a dog get on the farm?" Araba's mum questioned her dad.

"Probably Araba and Kofi have an explanation for that matter," Araba's daddy replied, looking at Araba and her younger brother Kofi.

"What do you mean? You are getting me worried", Araba's "mum said.

"Araba what's your daddy talking about? ". Araba's mummy asked? Araba pretended as if she had no clue about what was going on.

Another day went by Araba and her younger brother Kofi repeatedly faced a horrific and despicable ordeal by their (peers).

They did nothing to stop the bullying, neither they defended themselves, they were so helpless to do anything, it has been extremely obvious for their peers to take advantage as they had not yet reported it to any adults.

The puppy grew bigger and bigger as their parents were aware that both siblings had kept the puppy. The puppy was a full grown dog and became protective of Araba and her younger brother Kofi. Sometimes the dog goes out from the farmyard where Araba and her younger brother Kofi placed her.

The dog became aggressive towards anyone who dared threaten Araba and her younger brother Kofi, including their peers that picked on them.

As time went by the puppy who grew as a full grown dog became a comfort to Araba and her younger brother Kofi.

One sunny after-noon when Araba and Kofi were in school and their parents were busy working on the farm.

The dog walked across the farm through the bushes, chased bush animals across several fields and ended up in Araba and her younger brother Kofi's school.

The dog hid inside a garden where no-one could spot her near Araba and her younger brother Kofi, school.

Araba and her younger brother Kofi don't normally join their peers during play time due to the horrific and despicable act from their peers.

That after-noon both siblings put on a brave face and decided to go to the play field where all the childrens gathered and had fun.

Araba and her younger brother Kofi were scared to show their faces on the playground. Anytime they visit the playground they get picked on and bullied.

As the dog was in her hiding place in the garden near Araba and her younger brother's school, the dog could see everyone coming in and going out from the school.

As the dog became known to Araba and her younger brother school, the dog had followed Araba and her younger brother Kofi most often without them knowing, at school both had missed the prescence of the dog and they only wished they were with the dog at that moment.

It seems the two siblings at school always played by themselves, they were having more fun by themselves than ever, both laughing uncontrollably which upset those who were looking forward to bullying them.

Their moment of joy and freedom was brought to an end by their bullies, while there were no adults present at that moment.

The bullying peers walked over to where Araba and her younger brother Kofi were having a glorious moment and harassed them for laughing.

The two siblings did not utter a word; they stood there and watched their bullying peers harassing them till they were satisfied and left them on the playground shattered with fear.

Araba and younger brother Kofi returned to separate classrooms and joined the session, though they were in separate classrooms, both were shattered with fear after the incident on the playground.

When school was over Araba rushed to her younger brother Kofi's classroom, and asked Kofi if both can stay in the classroom until the whole place is clear.

Kofi asked Araba, why do you want us to stay here? " Araba replied, just to stay out of the bullies "sight", you know they won't leave us alone! Araba added.

However, no one was allowed to stay behind in the classroom when school was over, but Araba and her younger brother Kofi were scared of going out there. The caretaker in the school was doing usual routine when school was over.

They thought going out there just after school, they might run into their bullying peers, instead they want to stay behind to escape from the bullies.

Unfortunately, they couldn't hide any longer in the classroom as the caretaker saw them hiding in the classroom. Somehow they have to go out there and deal with the situation, but how?

Both siblings were not in the position to stop their peers from bullying them, lucky for them the dog got tired from hiding in the garden. The dog was aware Araba and her younger brother might still be in the school since they haven't come out from the school.

The bullying never stopped, this went on time and time, but Araba and her younger brother Kofi did what they always do to stay calm without fighting back.

The dog eventually came out from the garden near the school, hoping Araba and her younger brother Kofi would come out and walk home together with them.

School has been closed for over half an hour. Araba and her younger brother Kofi haven't been home yet, their parents at home are getting worried, it doesn't feel right. Araba and her younger brotherKofi are very punctual to get home when school is over.

Just before Araba and her younger brother Kofi decided to step out as the caretaker saw them, they also saw the dog rushing out from the nearby garden. Araba and her younger brother Kofi were very excited seeing the dog close.

Araba and her younger brother Kofi ran with joy towards the dog and embraced the dog with a heavy laugh. The caretaker screamed, hey kids what are you still doing here. This seems like a chance for the siblings to tell their sad story to the caretaker, but they couldn't.

Kofi asked Araba how did the dog get here?

Araba replied I don't know Kofi!

Both were surprised to see the dog coming out from the garden, suddenly" Araba, realized they were behind time since the school was over.

Araba said to Kofi. "Kofi" we have stayed longer than usual, we are behind time!

"Yes Araba" Kofi replied, mummy and daddy will get angry, what are we going to do? Said Araba.

Besides, we can't tell mummy and daddy anything about what happened on the playground. Araba, Kofi "called" we need to let daddy and mummy know. Kofi said!

No no no; Araba repeatedly cautioned Kofi, her younger brother, not to mention or say a word to their parents. But why, Kofi asked? Araba did not say anything; she was silent.

Araba, hesitating, broke her silence, and said you're right Kofi" we need to tell daddy and mummy.

Araba, knowing how busy their parents were, she thought for a minute and had a second thought and said to Kofi.

Please Kofi, we shouldn't tell daddy and mummy, but "why" Kofi asked Araba?

If we tell daddy and mummy we will make things worse for ourselves. What do you mean Araba?" said Kofi! Those bullies will get angry and make more trouble for us.

Oh I got it; Kofi exclaimed in surprise, and said to Araba, so what are we going to do?

Araba and her younger brother Kofi always get home on time when school is over. They've never wasted a minute of their time staying behind, both look worried, they've never been in trouble with their parents before.

At home the siblings' parents, still waiting patiently for them to come home, but no sign of both siblings.

This is not like them, why are they not yet at home, has something happened to them on the way, or are they still in the school, the siblings mother briefly asked their father? I don't know, the father replied.

Both parents were worried and terrified, assuming something terrible had happened to them on the way home.

The parents of the siblings sat quietly and consoling each other with very passionate words to calm the situation of Araba and her younger brother Kofi absent at home.

Araba's mum turned to Araba's dad and asked her dad, horny" Do you think the kids are ok? Do you think they will make it home?

Araba's dad looked at her mum with nice cheerful looks and replied to Araba's mum, darling, the kids will be fine and they will make it home as always I promised!

Though Araba's dad gave such an encouraging thought to Araba's mum, deep down he was not sure what might come of the situation, he tried to stay calm by Araba's mum's side, but deep down he was worried and terrified.

In the school, Araba and her younger brother Kofi unite with the dog, which was very amazing to Araba and her younger brother Kofi, during the most fearful moment in their life. However, both have no idea how they will explain the circumstance to their parents.

Meanwhile" Araba and her younger brother Kofi's bullying peers were not over with their lashing. After the school sessions were over.

Araba and her younger brother Kofi's bullying peers knew what they wanted to do to those defenseless siblings, they also waited for them to come out far from the school area and pounce on them like an eagle catching a bird.

However, Araba and her younger brother Kofi merged together with the dog and headed home. While heading home their bullying peers came out from nowhere attacking Araba and her younger brother Kofi.

During their attack on Araba and her younger brother Kofi, the dog rushed to their defense and scared the bullies off, the dog pounced on the bullies roar, barking and sniffed on the bullies to create a sense of mark identity.

Araba and her younger brother Kofi became relieved and ran home with the dog, the bullies were in shock and frightened, yet both siblings had no knowledge how they can explain to their parents about staying out for long after school sessions are over.

On the way home both siblings were troubled over how their parents would react if they couldn't give any lucrative explanation, the explanation was to tell them about the incident, but Araba was afraid to tell.

They thought hard to give some decent explanation to their parents to avoid any distress for both parents. The siblings have been terrorized for sometime now, and yet they can't find a way to break the fear and their silence to their parents or any adults.

The siblings and the dog walked home safely and merged with their parents. When Araba and her younger brother Kofi got home with the dog their parents were relieved.

Araba and her younger brother Kofi's mum ran to them and hugged them and said to them, why did you stay out for so long. This is where the question was supposed to begin, but just before Araba and her younger brother Kofi got home both siblings wasted no time.

Both siblings started with apologies to their parents, both said, dad and mum please forgive us this would not happen again.

Their parents, knowing the kind of kids, both parents, did not take into anger, they rather welcome them and caution them with a word of advice.

Both parents said to Araba and her younger brother Kofi, why did you stay out for so long. You got us worried, we thought something awful had happened to you both.

No, "mum" don't say that Araba replied with a selfless tone and paused. Kofi, her younger brother, then looked straight to Araba, hoping she would voice out the threat and the bullying and tell their parents about the bullies.

The dog was moving between Araba and her younger brother Kofi, wagging her tail. All along Araba's parents did not notice the absence of the dog in the farm, just because they are not used to dogs since they don't own one, and besides they were busy working.

Araba and her younger brother Kofi thought they would get into a big trouble when they got home, instead their parents humbly welcomed them passionately without questioning much why they were out there after the school session was over.

Dinner was ready over hours ago. You kids get ready and come to the table said Araba's mum. Araba and her younger brother Kofi went to get change and washed, then headed to the dining table.

The family gathered around the table, Araba's mum" started dishing the food and the family had a nice and quiet dinner with a lot of smiles on their faces behind the table.

After Araba and her family had finished their dinner all of them went to the sitting area, but before Araba had her dinner, they also set dinner for the dog in the dog bowl.

When they went to the sitting area, Araba asked, her younger brother Kofi had the dog "finished eating?" her younger brother Kofi replied! "I don't know Araba! Kofi and Araba ran to the corner where they set the dinner for the dog and checked on her.

The night went by the family once again united as usual and had a family fun in the sitting area together with the dog and the family finally retired to bed.

During the night Araba had a horrific nightmare whilst sleeping, her peers; were violently attacking her when walking the dog across a nearby field near a deep lake and small bridge over the lake.

While walking the dog, suddenly her peers showed up from nowhere and ran through the small bridge, violently attacking Araba. Her peers thought Araba was all alone on the bridge, but Araba and the dog were playing on the field when the dog suddenly spotted a bush animal and went after the bush animal who was snooping across the field, when her peers showed up trying to bully her.

The dog heard a scream, and rushed over to where the scream was coming from, and saw Araba was being attacked by the bullies. The dog immediately rushed to the bullies and stopped the bullies.

In Araba's dream she realized the dog would help them to overcome their bullies. She was very excited in the dream and thought she and her younger brother could do anything without being bothered by the bullies.

As the dog pounced on the bullies before, the bullies ceased to bother the siblings, but they never stopped there. They targeted other vulnerable kids and did the same horrible bullying like they did to Araba and her younger brother Kofi.

Yet the siblings couldn't report the bullying, the bullies put other kids through such a horrific ordeal. Araba and her younger brother Kofi, were much concerned about their parents' valuable time and they didn't want to involve them and waste their time and make things worse for themselves.

The siblings struggled to report the bullying, they kept quiet and allowed the bullies to abuse them emotionally with fears and violence, it is always the best to report bullying, prevention is always better than silence. When you report bullying you might also help others who are going through the same situation.

There Are many support centers where you can access and report bullying, we shouldn't let anyone go scot-free from bullying others, people bullying innocent adults and children and always get away without any repercussions, please ensure you can report bullying and inappropriate behaviors.

Araba and her younger brother Kofi, later had the courage from the grown up full big dog, and named the dog Hope, and the homeless wet and shivering puppy found home and helpless Araba and her younger brother Kofi found hope and happiness and became confident as the dog pounced on their bullies and never again the bullies bothered them.

Printed in the United States
by Baker & Taylor Publisher Services